18763205

I0576740

18763205

Haunted House Jokes

BY LOUIS PHILLIPS
Illustrated by James Marshall

PUFFIN BOOKS

SwC
J,
818.5402
Phil
12.95

For
Ian & Matthew Phillips
and
Spencer & Elizabeth Berger
Even when you are afraid,
it is good to keep your sense of humor.
L.P.

PUFFIN BOOKS
Published by the Penguin Group
Penguin Putnam Books for Young Readers,
345 Hudson Street, New York, New York 10014, U.S.A.
Penguin Books Ltd, 27 Wrights Lane, London W8 5TZ, England
Penguin Books Australia Ltd, Ringwood, Victoria, Australia
Penguin Books Canada Ltd, 10 Alcorn Avenue, Toronto, Ontario, Canada M4V 3B2
Penguin Books (N.Z.) Ltd, 182-190 Wairau Road, Auckland 10, New Zealand

Penguin Books Ltd, Registered Offices: Harmondsworth, Middlesex, England

First published in the United States of America by Viking Penguin Inc., 1987
Published in Puffin Books, 1988
Reissued 1999

1 3 5 7 9 10 8 6 4 2

Text copyright © Louis Phillips, 1987
Illustrations copyright © James Marshall, 1987
All rights reserved

THE LIBRARY OF CONGRESS HAS CATALOGED THE PREVIOUS PUFFIN EDITION UNDER CATALOG
CARD NUMBER: 88-42964
This edition ISBN 0-14-130650-5

Printed in the United States of America

Except in the United States of America, this book is sold subject to the condition that
it shall not, by way of trade or otherwise, be lent, re-sold, hired out, or otherwise
circulated without the publisher's prior consent in any form of binding or cover
other than that in which it is published and without a similar condition
including this condition being imposed on the subsequent purchaser.

RL: 2.5

CONTENTS

• CHAPTER ONE •
Dracula Hanging Out in the Attic   1
(You've got bats in your belfry!)

• CHAPTER TWO •
The Invisible Man in the Living Room   11
(That guy's outta sight!)

• CHAPTER THREE •
Ghosts in the Laundry Room   17
(Won't those sheets ever get clean?)

• CHAPTER FOUR •
Werewolves in the Den   27
(One more hair-raising experience!)

• CHAPTER FIVE •
Frankenstein's Monster in the Bedroom   35
(Who's that hiding under the bed?)

• CHAPTER SIX •
Skeletons in the Closet, Witches in the Kitchen   43
(Put down that broom. I have sweeping to do!)

• CHAPTER SEVEN •
Mummies in the Basement   53
(That wraps it up, folks!)

SWEETWATER COUNTY LIBRARY SYSTEM
SWEETWATER COUNTY LIBRARY
GREEN RIVER, WYOMING

CHAPTER ONE

Dracula Hanging Out in the Attic

(You've got bats in your belfry!)

Why does Dracula refuse to brush his teeth?
    He loves bat breath.

What happened when Dracula began to write poetry?
    He went from bat to verse.

What is Dracula's favorite animal?
    The giraffe.

What is Dracula's favorite snack at a football game?
    A fangfurter.

What did Dracula take for his cold?
    Coffin drops.

Knock, knock.
Who's there?
Snowman.
Snowman who?
　　Snowman. It's Dracula!

What did the math teacher say to Dracula?

    Count.

What is Dracula's favorite Christmas song?

    "I'm Screaming of a Bite Christmas."

What do you get if you cross Dracula with Sleeping Beauty?

    Tired blood.

Where does Dracula go swimming?

    In Lake Eerie.

Why is Dracula able to live so inexpensively?
　　He lives on necks to nothing.

Why does Dracula drink blood?
　　Champagne is too expensive.

LAUREN: What three words should you never say if you are being chased by Dracula?
NANCY: I give up.
LAUREN: Exactly.

What would Dracula be called if he won the national election held every four years in November?
　　President of the United States.

Why is Dracula the most unhappy of creatures?
　　Because he always loves in vein.

What's the difference between a person looking at Dracula and someone blinking?
　　One eyes a bat, while the other bats an eye.

Knock, knock.
Who's there?
Discount.
Discount who?
    Discount is named Dracula.

What position does Dracula play on the hockey team?
    Ghoulie.

Who is Dracula's hero?
    Batman, of course.

DRACULA: Good evening. Is this Stetner's Funeral Home?
VOICE ON THE PHONE: Yes, it is. May I help you?
DRACULA: Yes. Do you deliver?

Why did Dracula take his computer back to the factory?
    He wanted to improve its byte.

What has wings, fangs, is black on the inside and clear on the outside?
    A vampire in a Baggie.

MRS. WEREWOLF: What are you going to buy Dracula for his birthday?
MR. WEREWOLF: A batrobe.

DRACULA: What do people think about me?
MRS. DRACULA: They think you're a pain in the neck.

What is Dracula's favorite flavor of ice cream?
    Vein-illa.

What does Dracula use to build a prison?
    Blood cells.

The answer is: Count down
The question is: How does Dracula feel today?

What is Dracula's favorite television show?
    "Name That Tomb."

What is Dracula's favorite holiday?
    Fangsgiving.

What is Dracula's favorite fruit?
    Neck-tarines.

Why doesn't Dracula give up being a vampire?
    He can't. It's in his blood.

What is Dracula's favorite breed of dog?
    Bloodhound.

Why is Dracula such a big-time gambler?
    Because he has a lot at stake.

Where does Dracula do most of his singing?
    In the bat-tub.

*Why did the school nurse
  send Dracula home?*
        He had a coffin fit.

Louis: I had a fight with Dracula.
Jim: What happened?
Louis: He really chewed me out.

Why did Dracula do badly in school?
        He didn't have the right battitude.

What would happen if Dracula tried out for a movie?
        He'd get a bit part.

*What dance does Dracula perform when he goes to
Hawaii?*
        The DracHula.

Why did Dracula break up with his girlfriend?
        She wasn't his type (blood type, that is).

Why doesn't Dracula marry?
        He's a confirmed bat-chelor.

What will be the title of the new George Lucas movie about Dracula?
> "The Vampire Strikes Back."

Why wasn't Dracula allowed to play for the New York Yankees?
> He kept trying to get a hit with the wrong kind of bat.

Where does Dracula store his tools?
> In the bloodshed, of course.

What is Dracula's favorite sport?
> Bat-minton.

What happens in a vampire horse race?
> All the horses finish neck and neck.

Where in Arizona does Dracula go for a vacation?
> Tombstone.

What kind of reading does Dracula like best?
> Something in a light vein.

MATTHEW: Is it true that you can escape from Dracula if you carry a clove of garlic with you?
ELIZABETH: Yes, if you can carry the clove of garlic fast enough.

DRACULA: I just got a letter from the Invisible Man.

MRS. DRACULA: What does it say?

DRACULA: How should I know? He wrote it in invisible ink.

Knock, knock.
Who's there?
Avenue.
Avenue who?
　　　　Avenue ever heard of the Invisible Man?

THE INVISIBLE WOMAN: What was that terrible noise I heard last night?

THE INVISIBLE MAN: My sister fell down a long flight of stairs in the dark.

THE INVISIBLE WOMAN: Cellar?

THE INVISIBLE MAN: No, we'll keep her. She'll be all right.

MRS. DRACULA: Do you know that Frankenstein is going to marry the Invisible Woman?

DRACULA: I don't know what he sees in her.

BANDLEADER: What song do you want us to play at your surprise party for the Invisible Woman?

INVISIBLE MAN: "I Won't Be Seeing You in All the Old Familiar Places."

LANDLORD: How do you like your apartment as a whole?

THE INVISIBLE MAN: As a hole it's all right, but as an apartment it's terrible.

THE INVISIBLE WOMAN: How come the Creature from the Black Lagoon never comes to our parties?
THE INVISIBLE MAN: That creature is swamped with work.

THE INVISIBLE WOMAN: Why are you putting that 15-watt light bulb into the socket?
THE INVISIBLE MAN: The doctor told me to take a little light exercise.

Why is the Invisible Man so good at solving logic problems?
Because he's so clear-headed.

What do you get when you cross the Invisible Man with a jar of vanishing cream?

> What does it matter? Whatever you get, you won't be able to see it.

THE INVISIBLE MAN: I crossed the Atlantic Ocean twice and never took a bath.

THE BLOB: Why, you dirty double-crosser.

CHAPTER THREE
Ghosts in the Laundry Room
(Won't those sheets ever get clean?)

SWEETWATER COUNTY LIBRARY SYSTEM
SWEETWATER COUNTY LIBRARY
GREEN RIVER, WYOMING

What do ghosts use to clean their hair?
    ShamBoo.

What do ghosts call small minor bruises?
    Boo-boos.

What did the ghost in the tall grass of Indonesia cry?
    BamBOO! BamBOO!

What did the mother ghost tell her baby ghost at the dinner table?
    Quit goblin your food.

What did the sheet say to the ghost?
    Hold still. I've got you covered!

What do ghosts chew?
    Boo-ble gum.

BABY GHOST: Mommy, how did you and Daddy meet?
MOTHER GHOST: We met at a dance, and it was love at first fright.

Why do players hate to see ghosts at baseball games?
    Because all they do is BOO!

What do ghosts eat in Italy?
    Spookhetti.

What did the mother ghost tell her children when they got into the car?

Fasten your sheet-belts.

What do ghosts eat for breakfast?

Scream of wheat.

What do ghosts drink for breakfast?

Evaporated milk.

SPENCER: What is the difference between ghosts and snow?

LOU: I give up. What's the difference between ghosts and snow?

SPENCER: Ghosts come in sheets, while snow covers the ground with blankets.

What do ghosts drink in the summertime?
> Ghoul-ade.

What's the difference between a person who makes a losing bet, and a deserted mansion?
> One doesn't have a ghost of a chance, while the other has the chance of a ghost.

PAT: What did one ghost say to the other ghost?
IAN: I give up. What did one ghost say to the other ghost?
PAT: Do you believe in people?

What is white and powdery?
> Instant ghost.

What goes boo, putt putt putt; boo, putt putt putt?
    A ghost with an outboard motor.

Let's try that again. What goes boo, putt putt putt; boo, putt putt?
    A ghost playing golf.

One more for the road: What goes boo, putty, putty, putty; boo, putty, putty?
    A ghost replacing a broken window.

How did the kangaroo feel when she discovered she was carrying a ghost in her pouch?
    She was hopping mad.

What is white, then red, then white, then red, then white, then red, then white, etc.?

A ghost carrying a tomato and rolling down a hill with it.

Did the skeletons have a good time at the ghosts' Halloween party?

Yes, they had a rattlin' good time!

Why did the game warden in the forest arrest the ghost?

He had gone haunting without a license.

Why are ghosts so popular?
They raise everybody's spirits.

Where do ghosts go to get their mail?
To the dead letter office.

Are spooks and ghouls ever heard on the radio?
Of course—their programs are broadcast ghost
to ghost.

What did the ghost buy in the music store?
Sheet music, of course.

What did the baby spook do at the amusement park?
He took a ride on the roller-ghoster.

Why were the ghosts showing films underwater?
They wanted to go to a dive-in movie.

Who was the ghost's favorite movie actress?
        Boo Derek.

Who was the ghost's favorite movie actor?
        Scarey Grant.

FRANKENSTEIN'S MONSTER: Why do ghosts gather around the clothesline?
DRACULA: Oh, it's just a place to hang out.

Knock, knock.
Who's there?
Boo.
Boo who?
        Please don't cry.

Knock, knock.
Who's there?
Ice cream.
Ice cream who?
        Ice cream every time I see a ghost.

Why did the ghost bring up a baby skunk?
        He wanted to raise a stink.

CHAPTER FOUR

Werewolves in the Den

(One more hair-raising experience!)

HERMAN: Mother, all the children make fun of me.
MOTHER: What do they do?
HERMAN: They say I'm a werewolf. Is it true?
MOTHER: Of course it's not true. Now comb your face and get ready for supper.

THE BLOB: What kind of beans do you like for supper?
THE WEREWOLF: Human beans.

Why couldn't the werewolf use his car?
> Somebody let the hair out of his tires.

Why did the werewolf buy a pair of rabbits?
> He wanted a hare-raising experience.

Why does a werewolf sleep all day long?
    Who wants to wake him up?

What did the werewolf do after it was born?
    It ate the stork.

What do you call a werewolf who eats his father and mother?
    An orphan.

Why did the werewolf finally take a bath?
> He decided to give up his life of grime.

What do you do with a green werewolf?
> Thump him to see if he's ripe.

What is soft and mushy and found between a werewolf's teeth?
> Slow runners.

What was the werewolf's favorite musical?
> "Hair."

What do you call a werewolf who stands 8 feet tall and weighs 300 pounds?
> Sir.

THE BLOB: How was the werewolf's birthday party?
THE INVISIBLE MAN: It was a howling success.

DRACULA: Can you describe the experience of being a werewolf in four words?
WEREWOLF: Hair today, gone tomorrow.

What is the monster's favorite piece of classical music?
"Peter and the Werewolf."

What happened to the werewolf who ate Pinocchio for lunch?
He got splinters in his tongue.

What game do werewolves like to play when they get home from school?
Corpse and robbers.

What happened to the werewolf after he was run over by a steamroller?
Nothing. He just lay there with a long face.

DRACULA (*on the phone*): Operator, I want to talk to the werewolf who murdered all his friends.
OPERATOR: Is this a charge call?
DRACULA: No, make it poison to poison.

MRS. WEREWOLF: What game were you playing with Dr. Jekyll?

WEREWOLF, JR.: Hyde and seek.

WEREWOLF DEBORAH: What are you looking for in the newspaper?

WEREWOLF IVY: My horrorscope.

THE BLOB: Did you hear about the werewolf who ran away with the circus?

FRANKENSTEIN'S MONSTER: No. What happened?

THE BLOB: They made him give it back.

MAD SCIENTIST: What do you get when you cross a werewolf with an oak tree?

GHOST: I give up. What?

MAD SCIENTIST: A tree whose bark is as good as its bite.

MAD SCIENTIST: What do you call a neat, handsome, friendly, kind werewolf?

DRACULA: What?

MAD SCIENTIST: A failure.

THE ZOMBIE: I didn't realize that they put carpets on the beach.

WITCH: They didn't, silly. It's just five werewolves sunbathing.

What do you get when you cross a werewolf with a big yellow schoolbus?

A monster that seats 60 people.

What do you get when you cross a werewolf with Frankenstein's monster?

A crime wave.

CHAPTER FIVE

Frankenstein's Monster
in the Bedroom

(Who's that hiding under the bed?)

DRACULA: I think your Dr. Frankenstein built you upside down.
FRANKENSTEIN'S MONSTER: Why do you say that?
DRACULA: Because your feet smell and your nose runs.

THE INVISIBLE MAN: Why is Frankenstein's monster always complaining and coming up with wild ideas?
THE INVISIBLE WOMAN: Oh, the doctor keeps putting strange notions into his head.

Why is Dr. Frankenstein so muscular?
He's into body-building.

What does the Dr. Victor Frankenstein doll do?
It operates on batteries.

Why isn't Frankenstein's monster allowed inside a theater?
Because he insists on giving the actors a hand.

DRACULA: Did you hear that Dr. Frankenstein cloned his monster?

MRS. DRACULA: How does the monster feel?

DRACULA: Beside himself.

What has yellow skin, two legs, and a trunk?
Frankenstein's monster going on vacation.

FRANKENSTEIN'S MONSTER: I haven't seen my bride since we started to play that game four years ago!

DR. FRANKENSTEIN: What game?

FRANKENSTEIN'S MONSTER: Hide and seek.

TEACHER: Can you use the word *gruesome* in a sentence?

FRANKENSTEIN'S MONSTER: Between the ages of nine and ten, I gruesome.

FRANKENSTEIN'S MONSTER: Do you know what Dr. Frankenstein gave me for my birthday?

BRIDE OF FRANKENSTEIN: What?

FRANKENSTEIN'S MONSTER: A shirt with a very small collar.

BRIDE OF FRANKENSTEIN: How did you feel when you received the present?

FRANKENSTEIN'S MONSTER: All choked up.

FRANKENSTEIN'S MONSTER: Boy, is my wife angry with me.

DR. VICTOR FRANKENSTEIN: Why? What did you do now?

FRANKENSTEIN'S MONSTER: I opened a door for her.

DR. VICTOR FRANKENSTEIN: What's wrong with that?

FRANKENSTEIN'S MONSTER: It was a trapdoor.

What is Frankenstein's monster's favorite Christmas song?
"I'm Dreaming of a Fright Christmas."

Where does Frankenstein's monster sleep at night?
Anywhere he wants to.

What happened to Frankenstein's monster when he put dynamite in the refrigerator?
He blew his cool.

Why won't Frankenstein's monster read a book about a graveyard?
He doesn't like the plot.

IGOR: How is your new job as bill collector going?
CLIFF: Well, so many people refused to pay their bills that I hired Frankenstein's monster to go with me.
IGOR: Did it help?
CLIFF: Sure. People take one look at the monster and they hand the money right over to him.
IGOR: Then why do you look so sad?
CLIFF: *You* try to get the money away from the monster!

If Frankenstein's monster ran for President of the United States, why would he win?
He would get all the volts.

"Our knees feel stiff," said Frankenstein and his monster *jointly*.

MRS. DRACULA: Why was Frankenstein's monster late for our party?

DRACULA: He couldn't pull himself together in time.

BRIDE OF FRANKENSTEIN: Why didn't the decaying corpse come to our wedding party?

FRANKENSTEIN'S MONSTER: He felt rotten.

What goes CLOMP, squish, CLOMP, squish, CLOMP, squish?

       Frankenstein's monster wearing a wet tennis sneaker.

What did Frankenstein's monster do when he saw a shark swimming in his direction?

He fed him *Jaws*-breakers.

DR. FRANKENSTEIN: Stick out your tongue and say "Aah."
FRANKENSTEIN'S MONSTER: Why? I'm not angry with you.

FRANKENSTEIN'S MONSTER: You look like a million dollars.
BRIDE OF FRANKENSTEIN: Thank you.
FRANKENSTEIN'S MONSTER: Yeah, all green and wrinkled.

FRANKENSTEIN'S MONSTER: Doctor, what's your favorite sport?
DR. FRANKENSTEIN: Sleighing.
FRANKENSTEIN'S MONSTER: I mean, apart from business.

The answer is: club sandwich
The question is: What did Frankenstein's monster do to make his lunch hold still?

What acid played the monster in the Frankenstein movies?

> Boric Karloff.

FRANKENSTEIN'S MONSTER: Would you put yourself out for me?
DRACULA: Certainly.
FRANKENSTEIN'S MONSTER: Good, close the door behind you when you leave.

BRIDE OF FRANKENSTEIN: How many bones do you have in your body?
FRANKENSTEIN'S MONSTER: Over 900.
BRIDE OF FRANKENSTEIN: Over 900? Why, that's impossible.
FRANKENSTEIN'S MONSTER: No, it's not. I just ate a can of sardines for lunch.

FRANKENSTEIN'S MONSTER (*struggling to learn the English language*): I have went. That's not correct, is it?
DR. VICTOR FRANKENSTEIN: I have went? Of course it's not correct.
FRANKENSTEIN'S MONSTER: Why not?
DR. VICTOR FRANKENSTEIN: Because you haven't went yet!

CHAPTER SIX

Skeletons in the Closet, Witches in the Kitchen
(Put down that broom. I have sweeping to do!)

How many witches does it take to change a light bulb?
Only one—but she changes it into a frog.

THE GLOB: I understand that your friend joined the Navy.
THE BLOB: No, he's in the Ghost Guard.

What do you get if you cross a witch with a saxophone?
An instrument that plays a haunting melody.

WITCH DEBORAH: Do you want to go dancing tonight?
THE ZOMBIE: Not tonight, darling. I'm dead on my feet.

What do you call two witches living together?
     Broom-mates.

It is true that witches are not afraid of dead bodies?
     Of corpse.

Why do witches carry black cats on their brooms?
     Because elephants weigh too much.

THE BLOB: Boy, witches on broomsticks have terrible tempers.
THE GLOB: What do you mean?
THE BLOB: I mean they're always flying off the handle.

What did the mummy say when he got angry with the skeleton?

I have a bone to pick with you.

Knock, knock.
Who's there?
Witch.
Witch who?

Bless you!

WITCH: I would like to buy some alligator shoes.
SALESPERSON: Certainly, madam. What size shoe does your alligator wear?

Why wouldn't the witch buy a ticket to the spooks' auction?

She didn't have a ghost of a chance.

Why did the witch cross the road?

It was the chicken's day off.

When witches check into a hotel, what is the first thing they ask for?

Broom service.

THE BLOB: Gee, I'm thirsty. Could you make me a malted?
WITCH: Zap! You're a malted!

What did the witch say when she met the two-headed monster?
> Hello, hello. What's new, what's new?

Where do all the frightened people gather on Halloween?
> Witch-ita, Kansas.

WITCH: Why did you call the skeleton a coward?
THE BLOB: He has no guts.

Why do witches fly on brooms instead of vacuum cleaners?
> Because they can't find a vacuum cleaner with a long enough extension cord.

WITCH: What is Junior doing with that skeleton?
THE GLOB: He's boning up for his final exams.

Knock, knock.
Who's there?
Trigger.
Trigger who?
> Trigger Treat!

WITCH DEBORAH: Why is this Halloween picture of me in a hundred pieces?
THE BLOB PHOTOGRAPHER: I thought you asked me to blow it up!

WITCH FIFI: What do French skeletons say to their dining companions before every meal?
WITCH REGINA: What?
WITCH FIFI: Bone *appétit*.

WITCH KAREN: Why does your black cat go "Bow wow" instead of "Meow"?
WITCH DIANE: I'm trying to teach it a foreign language.

WITCH ALICE: Are you really going to marry Frankenstein's monster?
WITCH HAZEL: I was, but I'm beginning to experience grave doubts.

WITCH: How did you break your arm?

THE BLOB: I was raking leaves.

WITCH: I don't understand how you could break your arm while raking leaves.

THE BLOB: I fell out of the tree.

What did one witch's broom say to the other witch's broom?
> You swept me off my feet.

THE BLOB: How can you tell if there's a forty-foot monster under your bed?

WITCH ANNE: I give up. How can you tell if a forty-foot monster is under your bed?

THE BLOB: Your nose will be pressed against the ceiling.

Dr. Jekyll and Mr. Hyde: I'm adding glue to these aspirins.

The Blob: Why?

Dr. Jekyll and Mr. Hyde: Because I have a splitting headache.

Ian: Do you know the difference between a dozen witches and a dozen eggs?

Matthew: No, I don't.

Ian: Gee, that's too bad.

Matthew: Why?

Ian: Because I was going to send you to the store to buy a dozen eggs.

Witch #1: What's that costume you're wearing?

Witch #2: Oh, just something I dug up.

Chef: How do you like your eggs?

Witch: Terrifried.

And then there was the witch who placed a curse upon a man named Benny. She told him that if he ever used a razor on his face he would be turned into a large vase. Benny didn't pay any attention to the witch's curse, and one morning he got up and shaved himself. Sure enough—before he could sit down to breakfast, he was changed into a big vase. This goes to show you that *a Benny shaved is a Benny urned.*

How many witches does it take to change a light bulb?
None. Witches prefer the darkness.

CHAPTER SEVEN

Mummies in the Basement
(That wraps it up, folks!)

What would you get if you crossed a mummy with a porcupine?

A bandage with built-in air holes.

What is the mummy's favorite kind of music?

Ragtime, of course.

What's red and white on the outside and has yards and yards of bandages on the inside?

Campbell's Cream of Mummy Soup.

Which woman in the Haunted House became the wife of a United States President?
   Mummie Eisenhower.

How did the mummy lose so much weight?
   She went on a DIEt.

MUMMY #1: Where are you going tonight?
MUMMY #2: The ghosts have invited me to a reincarnation party.
MUMMY #3: What's a reincarnation party?
MUMMY #4: It's a come-as-you-were party.

MUMMY #1: Did you tell your girlfriend that when you looked into her eyes, time stood still?
MUMMY #2: Sort of.
MUMMY #1: What do you mean, sort of?
MUMMY #2: I told her that she had a face that would stop a clock.

DRACULA: Why didn't the mummy come to our Halloween party?

MRS. DRACULA: I guess he's all wrapped up in his work.

MUMMY #1: What would you do if you opened the front door and saw Dracula, Frankenstein's Monster, The Blob, three ghosts, a werewolf, and 12 witches standing on the doorstep?

MUMMY #2: Hope it was Halloween.

Why did the mummy keep his bandages in the refrigerator?
He used them for cold cuts.

What do the people of the United States send a needy mummy in Egypt?
A scare package.

What do you get when you cross a mummy with a vampire bat?
A flying Band-Aid.

What did the Egyptian say after finishing his work on the mummy?
That about wraps it up.

39092 04465331 1